This book belongs to:

_____

_____

_____

An Imprint of Sterling Publishing
387 Park Avenue South
New York, NY 10016

ISBN 978-0-7607-7070-2

Manufactured in Heshan, China
Lot #:
10 9

08/13

My Treasury of
CHRISTMAS
STORIES

Sandy Creek
NEW YORK

Contents

The First Christmas

Our story begins in old Nazareth,
where a young maiden, Mary, was to marry Joseph.
But one day the angel Gabriel appeared,
saying to Mary, "There is nothing to be feared.
You have been chosen to bear God's son.
His name will be Jesus. He will save everyone."

Mary was worried. What would Joseph say
if she was with child on their wedding day?
But Gabriel gave Joseph the wondrous news
that she bore God's son, the King of the Jews.
So Mary and Joseph were happily married,
and awaited the child that sweet Mary carried.

Then one day a messenger came to declare
they should go to their birthplace to pay taxes there.
Mary rode her donkey while Joseph led them
on the long winding road toward Bethlehem.
They journeyed on, all day until night,
when, finally, Bethlehem came into sight.

As they entered the town, it soon became clear
that they needed to rest, for the baby was near.
But wherever they went, they were told the same thing:
"Sorry, we're full. There's no room at the inn."
"I have a small stable," one innkeeper said.
"It's warm and it's dry, with clean straw for a bed."

So that very night, before break of dawn,
the animals watched as Jesus was born.
They all rejoiced as they saw, where he lay,
God's only son, in a manger of hay.
They did not know that the baby so small
would one day grow up to save us all.

High over the hills, on that joyous night,
some shepherds were roused by a dazzling light.
"Do not be afraid," an angel said,
"I've come with good tidings God wants you to spread.
Born on this night is a baby boy
who'll bring peace on Earth, goodwill, and joy."

When darkness returned and the shepherds were able,
they left their sheep flocks and went to the stable.
They knelt before Jesus and began to sing,
"Praise be to God for our Savior, the King."
Then they told Mary all they had heard,
before they departed to spread the good word.

In a land to the east, over hills afar,
three wise men saw a bright new star.
The wise men knew that the star foretold
the birth of a King, for it was written of old.
And so they journeyed night after night,
following the star that shone so bright.

At last they arrived in Jerusalem town,
where King Herod sat on the throne in his crown.
They asked him, "Have you seen the new Jewish King?
We've followed the star in search of him."
Herod was angry, for he was no fool;
he knew that a new king would threaten his rule.

He said, "When you find the King of the Jews,
return by my palace to pass on the news."
So, bearing rich gifts, they went on to find
the little Lord Jesus, so gentle and kind.
Kneeling before him, they started to sing,
"With these precious gifts, we praise the new King."

But that silent night, as the wise men dreamed,
God told them that Herod was not what he seemed.
"King Herod is filled with jealousy,
and he means to have Jesus killed heartlessly.
So listen well to this warning I say,
and journey home by another way."

Then an angel appeared to Joseph one night,
to tell him his family should also take flight.
"Hark," sang the angel, "pack up and flee
to the land of Egypt till God calls unto thee."
So Jesus was saved to teach of God's glory,
and that is the end of the first Christmas story.

A
Christmas
Carol

One Christmas Eve, in old London town,
Ebenezer Scrooge looked out with a frown.
"Merry Christmas, Uncle!" called his cheery nephew.
"Come join in our festive dinner, won't you?"
"Bah, humbug," growled Scrooge, "to Christmas Day!
What's merry about it? Now just go away!"

Poor Cratchit, his clerk, who worked hard each day,
asked Scrooge, "Is tomorrow a holiday?"
"I suppose you will want me to pay you as well!"
grumbled Scrooge, who was stingy as you can tell.
Scrooge hated Christmas because he was greedy.
He felt no pity for the poor and the needy.

Later that evening, when Scrooge was alone,
he heard rattling chains and a ghostly moan.
Then Scrooge saw poor Marley, who in happier days
was Scrooge's partner with the same selfish ways.
"Scrooge," wailed the ghost, "I've come to warn thee,
mend your greedy ways, or you'll end up like me.

"Deep in the night, before Christmas Day,
three Spirits will come to show you the way."
With that, Marley's ghost then started to fade,
leaving Ebenezer Scrooge alone and afraid.
Scrooge was dismayed as he crept into bed.
But he drifted to sleep, despite his great dread.

As the clock struck one on that freezing night,
Ebenezer Scrooge awoke with a fright.
And as he blinked his eyes in the gloom,
an unearthly Spirit appeared in the room.
"Follow me," it said, as Scrooge looked aghast.
"I am the Ghost of Christmas Past!"

The ghost took Scrooge back to Christmases of old,
when Scrooge was warm-hearted, not sad and cold.
They saw Fan, his sister, and Fezziwig his boss.
"I was happy," gasped Scrooge, "not lonely and cross."
And as Scrooge was shown each old Christmas day,
he cried, "I can't bear it! Take me away!"

In the blink of an eye, Scrooge returned to his bed,
and was met by a jolly spirit who said,
"I am the good Ghost of Christmas Present.
Follow me now to see something pleasant."
In a flash, they were in Bob Cratchit's place,
which looked very festive, despite the cramped space.

Scrooge watched the Cratchits sit down to eat
their small Christmas dinner as if a great treat.
"God Bless us, every one," Tiny Tim cried,
as his family blessed him, smiling with pride.
"Tiny Tim," said the Spirit, "will always be lame.
But he is still cheerful, despite his great pain."

As the Spirit departed, another took shape—
a horrible creature in a hood and a cape.
It spoke not a word and seemed to be dumb.
It was the Ghost of Christmas Yet to Come.
At the graveyard it showed Scrooge what lay ahead:
misery and sorrow for Tiny Tim was dead.

Then Scrooge saw his own grave, unloved and unkept,
alone in a cemetery where nobody wept.
As they wandered the streets, he heard people say,
"The old miser's gone, but who cares anyway?"
As the ghost disappeared Scrooge did something strange:
he fell down and wept, "Now I know I must change!"

The very next moment, Scrooge woke in his bed.
He raced to the window, then joyfully said,
"I haven't missed Christmas—what wonderful fun.
Merry Christmas," he called out, "to everyone!"
Then he stopped a small boy and asked humbly,
"Please take this turkey to the Cratchit family."

Then, handing out gifts, he tramped through the chill,
to call on his nephew and wish him goodwill.
And so began a most wonderful day,
full of laughter and joy, feasting and play.
Scrooge had been taught, as we hoped he would,
not to be stingy, but giving and good!

The Night Before Christmas

Twas the night before Christmas,
when all through the house
Not a creature was stirring, not even a mouse.
The stockings were hung by the chimney with care,
In hope that St. Nicholas soon would be there.

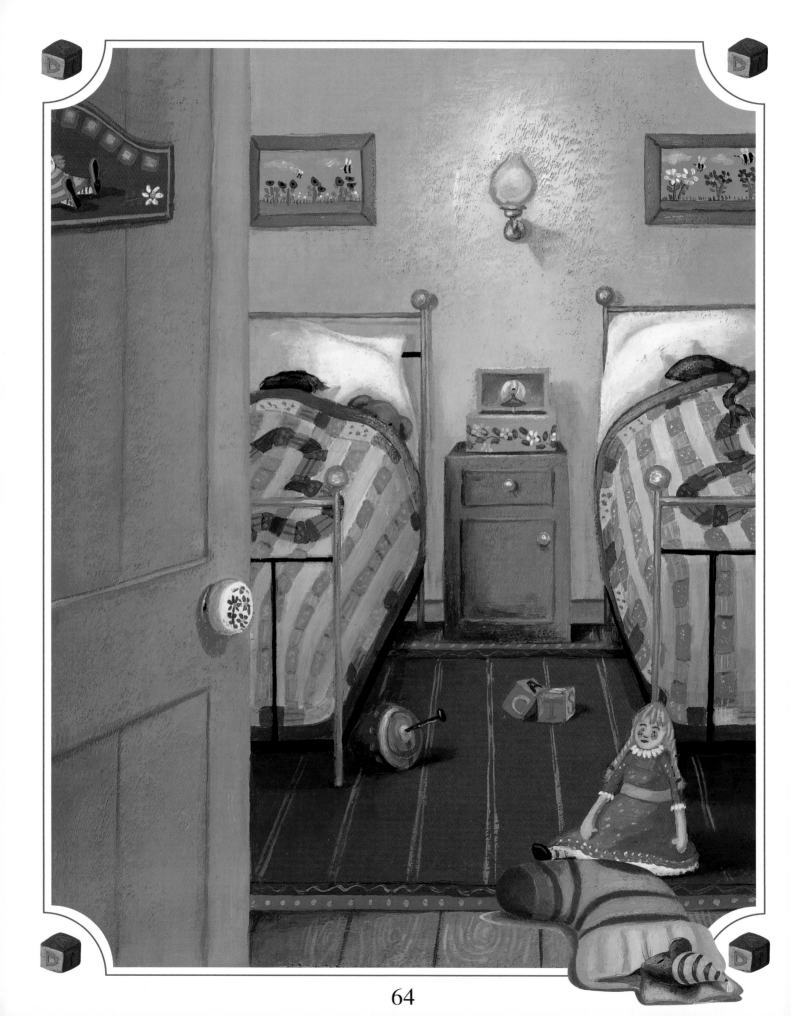

The children were nestled all snug in their beds,
While visions of sugarplums danced in their heads;
And Mama in her kerchief and I in my cap,
Had just settled down for a long winter's nap.
When out on the lawn there arose such a clatter,
I sprang from the bed to see what was the matter.

Away to the window I flew like a flash,
Tore open the shutters and threw up the sash.
The moon on the breast of the new-fallen snow
Gave luster of midday to objects below,
When, what to my wondering eyes should appear,
But a miniature sleigh and eight tiny reindeer.

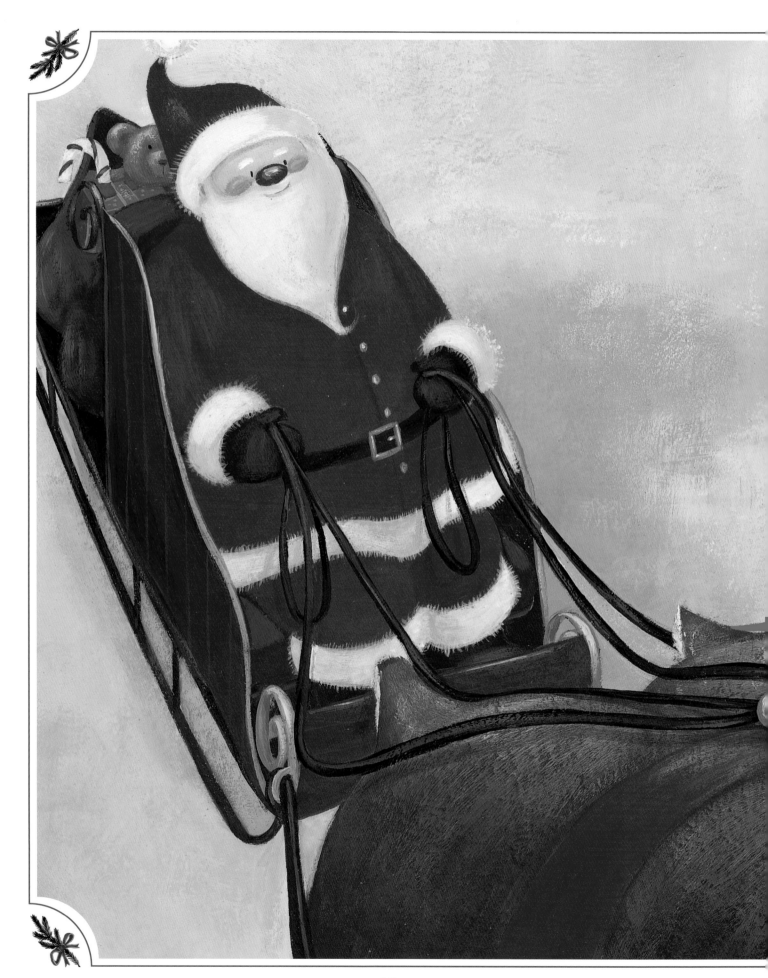

With a little old driver so lively and quick,
I knew in a moment it must be St. Nick.
More rapid than eagles his coursers they came,
And he whistled and shouted
and called them by name;

"Now Dasher! Now Dancer! Now Prancer and Vixen!
On Comet! On Cupid! On Donner and Blitzen!
To the top of the porch! To the top of the wall!
Now dash away! Dash away! Dash away all!"

As dry leaves that before the wild hurricane fly,
When they meet with an obstacle, mount to the sky,
So up to the housetop the coursers they flew,
With a sleigh full of toys and St. Nicholas too.
And then in a twinkling, I heard on the roof
The prancing and pawing of each little hoof.

As I drew in my head, and was turning around,
Down the chimney St. Nicholas came with a bound.
He was dressed all in fur, from his head to his foot,
And his clothes were all tarnished with ashes and soot.
A bundle of toys he had flung on his back,
And he looked like a pedlar just opening his pack.

75

His eyes—how they twinkled! His dimples—how merry!
His cheeks were like roses, his nose like a cherry!
His droll little mouth was drawn up like a bow,
And the beard of his chin was as white as the snow.

The stump of a pipe he held tight in his teeth,
And the smoke it encircled his head like a wreath.
He had a broad face and a little round belly,
That shook when he laughed, like a bowlful of jelly.

He was chubby and plump, a right jolly old elf,
And I laughed when I saw him, in spite of myself.
A wink of his eye and a twist of his head,
Soon gave me to know I had nothing to dread.

He spoke not a word, but went straight to his work,
And filled all the stockings; then turned with a jerk,
And laying his finger aside of his nose
And giving a nod, up the chimney he rose.

He sprang to his sleigh, to his team gave a whistle,
And away they all flew like the down of a thistle.
But I heard him exclaim ere he drove out of sight,
"Merry Christmas to all, and to all a goodnight!"

The
Nutcracker

One cold and frosty Christmas Eve night,
the Stahlbaum house shone festive and bright.
Twinkling candles lit up the tree
as guests arrived for the Stahlbaums' party.
Clara and Fritz both clapped to see treats
of chocolate, candy canes, sugar mice, and sweets.

The last to arrive was Herr Drosselmeyer,
who offered his gifts for all to admire.
Clara and Fritz chuckled and cheered,
as two life-size dolls suddenly appeared.
Then Clara and Fritz watched, entranced,
as the magical dolls whirled and danced.

Then Herr Drosselmeyer took out the best gift of all:
he gave Clara a splendid Nutcracker doll.
In his elegant uniform he was a fine sight,
and Clara's eyes opened wide with delight.
But before Clara's thanks had even been spoken,
Fritz grabbed the doll and it was broken!

Herr Drosselmeyer, being kindly and good,
tried mending the Nutcracker's splintered wood.
Then, after much feasting, dancing, and play,
Herr Drosselmeyer left on his sleigh.
As they waved good night, Clara's mother said,
"Hurry now, children, it's time for bed."

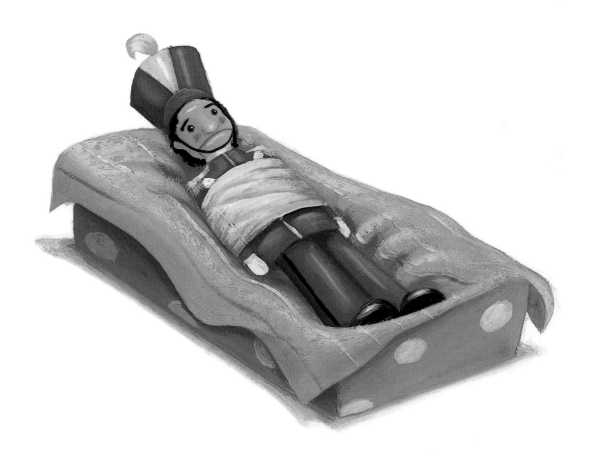

Later that night, as the silent house slept,
Clara rose from her bed and down the stairs crept.
Then among all the presents she quickly sought
the Nutcracker that Herr Drosselmeyer brought.
Snuggling down with the doll at her chest,
she waited for sweet dreams to fill her night's rest.

Before very long she awoke with a fright,
startled by strange sounds in the still night.
Sitting up quickly and blinking her eyes,
she saw that the toys had grown to life size!
Her beloved Nutcracker stood mighty and tall.
When she stood beside him, Clara felt small!

Behind him tin soldiers stood in a row,
with their muskets all loaded and ready to go.
Then a troop of gray mice marched into the room
and started a battle by the light of the moon.
The mighty mouse army, led by the Mouse King,
bombarded the soldiers and looked set to win.

The Nutcracker commanded as best he could,
but they were outnumbered—it didn't look good.
When the Nutcracker fell, Clara took up her shoe,
and aimed at the Mouse King, then desperately threw.
The soldiers all cheered as the King was struck down.
The mice were defeated, and the toys seized his crown.

When Clara looked into the Nutcracker's eyes
she was amazed, and gasped with surprise.
For during the battle, or perhaps even since,
he had changed from a doll to a handsome young prince!
Now the prince looked at Clara, bowed down, and cried,
"Come, my dear Clara, let's go outside!"

The prince led Clara to a magical sleigh
that flew through the night to a land far away.
There, beneath the stars twinkling bright,
enchanted snowflakes danced through the night.
"The dance is for you," the handsome prince said.
"But we mustn't stop here, there's more fun ahead."

They journeyed on to the Kingdom of Sweets,
a land full of dancing and sugary treats.
The Sugar Plum Fairy, so dainty and nice,
danced especially for Clara on a stage of ice.
Next came a dance from the sweets of the world,
who made Clara dizzy as they twisted and twirled.

The next thing she knew, Clara was awoken
and her Nutcracker doll was no longer broken.
Had her adventure been all that it seemed,
or was it a fantasy she had just dreamed?
Clara's questions were soon chased away
as Fritz wished her a Merry Christmas Day!

The Twelve Days of Christmas

On the first day of Christmas
my true love gave to me
a partridge in a pear tree.

On the second day of Christmas
my true love gave to me
two turtle doves
and a partridge in a pear tree.

On the third day of Christmas
my true love gave to me
three French hens,
two turtle doves
and a partridge in a pear tree.

On the fourth day of Christmas
my true love gave to me
four calling birds,
three French hens,
two turtle doves
and a partridge in a pear tree.

On the fifth day of Christmas
my true love gave to me
five gold rings,
four calling birds,
three French hens,
two turtle doves
and a partridge in a pear tree.

On the sixth day of Christmas
my true love gave to me
six geese a-laying,
five gold rings,
four calling birds,
three French hens,
two turtle doves
and a partridge in a pear tree.

On the seventh day of Christmas
my true love gave to me
seven swans a-swimming,
six geese a-laying,
five gold rings,
four calling birds,
three French hens,
two turtle doves
and a partridge in a pear tree.

On the eighth day of Christmas
my true love gave to me
eight maids a-milking,
seven swans a-swimming,
six geese a-laying,
five gold rings,
four calling birds,
three French hens,
two turtle doves
and a partridge in a pear tree.

On the ninth day of Christmas
my true love gave to me
nine ladies dancing,
eight maids a-milking,
seven swans a-swimming,
six geese a-laying,
five gold rings,
four calling birds,
three French hens,
two turtle doves
and a partridge in a pear tree.

On the tenth day of Christmas
my true love gave to me
ten lords a-leaping,
nine ladies dancing,
eight maids a-milking,
seven swans a-swimming,
six geese a-laying,
five gold rings,
four calling birds,
three French hens,
two turtle doves
and a partridge
in a pear tree.

On the eleventh day of Christmas
my true love gave to me
eleven pipers piping,
ten lords a-leaping,
nine ladies dancing,
eight maids a-milking,
seven swans a-swimming,
six geese a-laying,
five gold rings,
four calling birds,
three French hens,
two turtle doves
and a partridge
in a pear tree.

On the twelfth day of Christmas
my true love gave to me
twelve drummers drumming,
eleven pipers piping,
ten lords a-leaping,
nine ladies dancing,
eight maids a-milking,
seven swans a-swimming,
six geese a-laying,
five gold rings,
four calling birds,
three French hens,
two turtle doves
and a partridge
in a pear tree.

The Little Fir-tree

eep in the forest, quite hidden from view
among the tall pines, a small fir-tree grew.
The taller trees laughed when they heard the fir moan,
"I wish I were taller, I can't wait 'til I'm grown!"
"The forest is fun," the small fir-tree was told.
"Live for the moment. Don't wish to be old."

Two winters passed, then trees were chopped down,
trimmed of their branches and taken to town.
"Where are they going?" the little tree wails.
"They're off to the ocean to hold up some sails."
"Oh, I wish I were taller," the small fir-tree sighed.
"Then I'd be a proud mast and sail far and wide."

Soon it was Christmas and men came around
to dig the tall fir-trees from the frozen ground.
"Now those trees are special," a small robin cried.
"They're decked out in baubles and taken inside."
"Oh my, what an honour," the small fir-tree said.
"Rather than sailing, I'll do that instead."

Another year passed and Christmas Eve dawned.
"The woodsmen are coming," the early bird warned.
"Oh my, what a beauty," the old woodsman cried,
and dug up the small fir-tree, who trembled with pride.
"At last," sighed the fir-tree, as he left the warm earth.
"The time has arrived to show what I'm worth."

But when he was leaving, he didn't feel glad.
Instead he felt tearful and terribly sad.
He called to the birds, the rabbits and deer
and all of the friends that he'd grown up so near.
And with that farewell, he was carried away,
and thrown on the back of a bumpy old sleigh.

149

Arriving at a grand house beneath the full moon,
the fir-tree was put in a magnificent room.
Decked out with tinsel, and finished with bows,
the fir-tree was splendid from his head to his toes.
The children clapped and shouted with glee,
as the fir-tree stood proudly – a tall, handsome tree.

On Christmas day, from his green boughs,
children picked presents for hours and hours.
Then there was dancing, feasting and drink.
The tree was so happy, he started to think,
"My new friends adore me and seem very kind."
He forgot to feel sad that he'd left friends behind.

And as day turned to evening, a story was told,
that dazzled the fir-tree with deeds brave and bold.
When it was over he swayed with delight,
as the room emptied with calls of goodnight.
"What joy," thought the fir-tree. "I'm glad that I came.
I can't wait 'til tomorrow for more of the same."

The proud fir-tree thought, "This is where I belong."
But when morning dawned it seemed he was wrong.
Dragged from the fine room, he was bundled away
and thrust in an old shed with no light of day.
Then out of the darkness, he heard something squeak,
he felt his twigs rustle, heard the patter of feet.

"Hello," said a white mouse. "Why are you here?
Tell us your story as we see in the New Year."
And so he told tales of his youth long ago,
of the birds, the animals, and the deep, crispy snow.
As the mice gasped in wonder at all he had done,
the tree understood that the forest had been fun.

And so the tree slumbered away in the shed,
dreaming of forests and fresh air, instead,
until he was shaken awake by the noise
of children who'd come in search of their toys.
"Look it's our fir-tree," a little voice cried.
"Let's shake off the dust and plant it outside."

And from that beginning, much to his surprise,
the fir-tree grew strong and terribly wise.
Now down in the garden the big fir-tree grows,
spreading the wisdom of all that he knows.
"Youth is a blessing and nature is best.
Live for the moment, and not for the rest."

The
Snow Queen

Gather round children, I've a tale to tell.
It begins with a mirror and a terrible spell.
The mirror was cursed by a demon so mean
that he wished to spread sorrow wherever he'd been.
The mirror, you see, would show only bad,
so all who gazed in it looked ugly and sad.

As the foul demon flew with the mirror up high,
it slipped from his hands and fell through the sky.
It shattered to Earth, and folk cried in surprise
as splinters stabbed at their hearts and their eyes.
Then they grew cold and knew kindness no more,
but felt only spite for whoever they saw.

In a distant land, full of laughter and joy,
lived Gerda and Kay, a young girl and boy.
Whatever the season, they met every day—
two little friends who just loved to play.
Outside their doors they each grew a rose,
which, just like their friendship, never wilted nor froze.

When it was frosty, they hid from the cold,
while Granny told folk tales from ages of old.
"Beware, dear children, of the chilly Snow Queen,
for she spreads only coldness whenever she's seen."
Gerda was frightened, but Kay sat up tall,
and promised he'd guard her from one and all.

But one winter's day, Kay let out a cry,
"There's a stab in my heart and a pain in my eye!"
It seems that some mirror had fallen on him.
From that moment on he was grumpy and grim.
He snatched up his sled and hurried away.
Gerda asked where he was going, but Kay wouldn't say.

When a white sleigh swept past, Kay hitched a ride.
Then up through the air he felt his sled glide.
Faster and faster, they sped over the land,
till they reached a snow palace icy and grand.
"Come," said a voice that was cold and serene.
And little Kay gasped—it was the Snow Queen!

When he didn't return by dawn the next day,
Gerda jumped in a boat and went searching for Kay.
She found an enchantress and told of her quest.
The enchantress commanded, "Stay here as my guest."
Gerda's sadness vanished till one sunny day,
some bright blooming roses made her think of Kay.

"Caw!" called a raven. "I'll help you find Kay.
He's married a princess—I'll show you the way."
But he was mistaken, the prince was another—
not the young boy she loved as a brother.
The prince and his princess, so happy in marriage,
sent Gerda away with warm clothes and a carriage.

But as she drove on, she heard a wild shout,
and feared for her life as robbers leaped out.
In the gang's castle, Gerda trembled and cried.
Then a robber-girl came and knelt by her side.
Quietly she whispered, "I'll let you go free.
Here, take my reindeer and quickly flee."

And so they galloped all through the night
to a land where the snow was sparkling white.
"Fear not," said the reindeer. "Help is at hand.
I know a wise woman who lives in this land."
And when they asked her, she showed them the way
that Kay had ridden on the big, white sleigh.

Meanwhile, to the north, on that chilly night,
Kay sat in the palace so icy and bright.
The Snow Queen had turned Kay's heart into ice.
He'd forgotten Gerda and everything nice.
"Kay," breathed the Snow Queen, "now listen to me,
just solve this ice puzzle, and you can go free."

Kay did not notice as Gerda rushed in.
But she did not falter, she just cuddled him.
As Gerda's warm tears fell on Kay's chest,
they thawed the heart of the friend she loved best.
"I'm free!" gasped Kay, as he slowly unfroze.
"I've solved the puzzle—it is an ice rose!"

"Come with me," laughed Gerda. "It's time to go."
And riding the reindeer, they sped through the snow.
Gerda waved and thanked all the friends that she saw,
until they arrived at a rose-covered door.
"Grandma," shouted Kay, "it's great to be home,
I promise from this day that I'll never roam."

The End